Jazz Baby

by Carole Boston Weatherford

illustrated by Laura Freeman

Lee & Low Books Inc. ♪ New York

LEE & LOW BOOKS Inc., 95 Madison Avenue, New York, NY 10016
leeandlow.com

Manufactured in China
Book design by Mina Greenstein   Book production by The Kids at Our House
The text is set in Veljovic Medium.
The illustrations are rendered digitally using a computer program that replicates
the look of pastel chalks.

  2 3 4 5 6 7 8 9 10 (HC)   (PB) 10 9 8 7 6 5 4 3 2 1
First Edition

Library of Congress Cataloging-in-Publication Data
Weatherford, Carole Boston.
Jazz baby / by Carole Boston Weatherford ; illustrated by Laura Freeman.— 1st ed.
   p.   cm.
Summary: A group of toddlers move and play, hum and sleep to a jazz beat.
ISBN 1-58430-039-6 (hardcover)   ISBN 1-58430-273-9 (paperback)
[1. Toddlers—Fiction. 2. Jazz—Fiction. 3. Stories in rhyme.] I. Freeman, Laura, ill. II. Title.
PZ8.3.W374 Jaz 2002   [E]—dc21   2001029796

ISBN-13: 978-1-58430-039-7 (hardcover)   ISBN-13: 978-1-58430-273-5 (paperback)

To the new jazz baby in the family. Welcome!
—C.B.W.

To Griffin, my Jazz Baby.
—L.F.

Jazz baby, jazz baby,
join the band.
You've got music
in your hands.

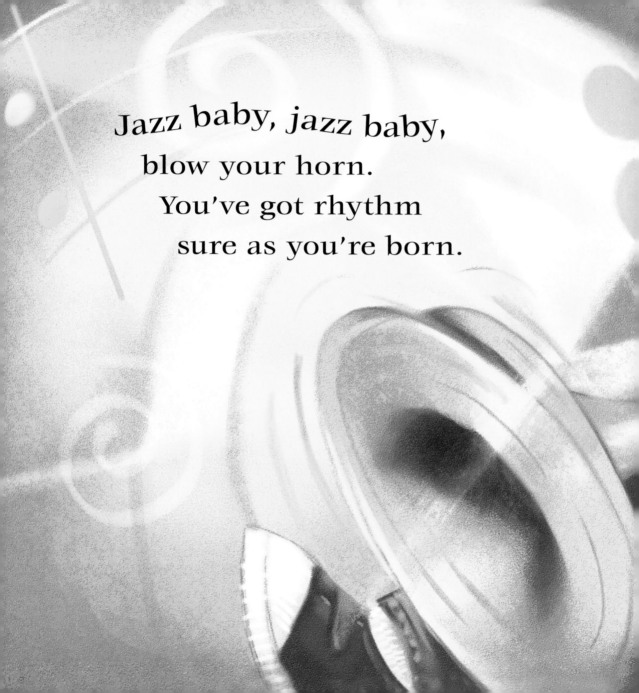

Jazz baby, jazz baby,
blow your horn.
You've got rhythm
sure as you're born.

Jazz baby, jazz baby,
tap your feet.
Snap your fingers,
happy beat.

Jazz baby, jazz baby,
pound your drum.
Hear it thump, thump,
rum-a-tum-tum.

Jazz baby, jazz baby,
swing and sway.
Shake and shimmy,
dance all day.

Jazz baby, jazz baby,
strike those keys.
Make them plink, plink
if you please.

Jazz baby, jazz baby,
cut a rug.
Jiggle, wiggle,
jitterbug.

Jazz baby, jazz baby,
pluck those strings.
Till that big bass
sizzles, sings.

Jazz baby, jazz baby,
hippity hop.
Bounce and boogie,
bebop-de-bop.

Jazz baby, jazz baby,
hum a song.
Let it rock you
all night long.